THE MONKEY KING
Wreaks Havoc in Heaven

Based on *Journey to the West*

by Wu Cheng'en

New Translation by Li Chaoyuan

Illustrations by Lu Xinsen & Yan Dingxian

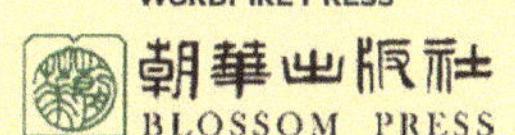

WFP
WORDFIRE PRESS

朝華出版社
BLOSSOM PRESS

EBook ISBN: 978-1-68057-479-1
Trade Paperback ISBN: 978-1-68057-480-7
Hardcover ISBN: 978-1-68057-481-4

Cover design by Janet McDonald
Adapted by Firethorn
Review by Scott Huntsman
Edited and Adapted by Rebecca Moesta
Published by
WordFire Press, LLC
PO Box 1840
Monument CO 80132

Kevin J. Anderson & Rebecca Moesta, Publishers
WordFire Press eBook Edition 2022
WordFire Press Trade Paperback Edition 2022
WordFire Press Hardcover Edition 2022
Printed in the USA

Join our WordFire Press Readers Group for
sneak previews, updates, new projects, and giveaways.

Sign up at wordfirepress.com

REVIEW

Previously, we learned about the Monkey King's birth.

After earth and sky separated, a rock on Flowers and Fruit Mountain in the Aolai Kingdom on the Eastern Continent was nourished by the sun and moon until it acquired supernatural powers. One day, it burst open and produced a stone monkey. The stone monkey was brave enough to pass through a waterfall and discover Water Curtain Cave, which won him the respect of all monkeys and the title of Monkey King.

Seeking to learn the secret of immortality, the Monkey King traveled to the Western Continent and became a student of Master Puti. The Master gave him the name Sun Wukong and taught him remarkable skills, such as the seventy-two transformations, the cloud-somersault, and other spells. The Master banished Wukong, however, for showing off his skills to his fellow students.

When the Monkey King returned to his tribe, he found out that it had been raided by the Demon King of Chaos. Outraged that his cave had been plundered, the Monkey King killed the Demon King and revitalized Flowers and Fruit Mountain. To reinforce his defenses, Wukong stole countless weapons from the capital of the Aolai Kingdom and trained his subjects to practice kung fu with them.

Earlier, while pursuing immortality, the Monkey King studied with Master Puti and learned many remarkable skills from him. When Wukong returned to Flowers and Fruit Mountain, he trained his subjects in kung fu with weapons.

One day during their routine drills, the Monkey King joined the monkeys on the martial arts field and put on an amazing display with his ringed broadsword. Wukong's curved sword flashed in the light, streaking as fast as a meteor across the sky. Impressed, the monkey soldiers applauded.

Suddenly, with a *clink*, his sword snapped into two pieces. The Monkey King was very upset.

"Your Majesty, you are an immortal sage now, and ordinary weapons are not fit for you anymore," suggested an old ape. "The water that flows under our iron bridge leads directly to the Water Crystal Palace of the Eastern Ocean Dragon king. Why not go there and ask the Dragon King for a divine weapon?"

The Monkey King was delighted. "Wait for me—I'll go there!"

He jumped to the end of the bridge, made a magic sign, and plunged in. The spell pushed the water aside to make a path on the ocean floor for Wukong, and he headed straight to the Water Crystal Palace of the Eastern Ocean Dragon King.

He arrived in almost no time.

When the Dragon King of the Eastern Ocean heard from his guards about the Monkey King's arrival, he hurried to the palace entrance with his children, grandchildren, prawn soldiers, and crab generals to greet their visitor.

After some small talk, the Monkey King revealed the intentions of his visit. "Once I became immortal, I returned to train my subjects and defend my cave. Unfortunately I have never had a proper weapon, so I came to you, my old neighbor, to see if you could give me one."

Unable to refuse, the Dragon King asked his Captain Mackerel and Porter Eel to bring out a nine-pronged fork weighing 3,600 pounds for the Monkey King. Wukong picked it up and complained that it was too light. The Dragon King then ordered his Colonel Bream and Commander Carp to bring a halberd weighing 7,200 pounds. The Monkey King tried a few thrusts and claimed that it was also too light.

"My honorable sage guest, this is the heaviest weapon in my palace," said the dismayed Dragon King. "I have nothing better."

Wukong did not believe it.

Minister Turtle noticed and cautioned the Dragon King in a low voice. "Your Majesty, this is no ordinary monkey. We do have a piece of precious magic iron in our palace. It started glowing brightly over the last few days. Could it be because of him?"

The Dragon King nodded. He took the Monkey King to the center of the ocean above a treasure chamber. He pointed down into the depths, where golden rays shone from a storehouse. "That light is the precious magic iron used to stabilize the oceans. If you can lift it, it is yours."

Wukong hurried to it.

The rare piece of iron was in the form of a staff, more than six meters tall and as thick as a barrel. Finding it too heavy to move, the Monkey King said, "I wish it were shorter and thinner." The magic iron heard him and instantly became smaller. Wukong was pleased. When he pulled it off the sea floor with great force, an earthquake shook Water Crystal Palace.

Everyone was frightened and hid.

The Monkey King was very happy with the treasure. He finally found the opportunity to inspect it closely. It was in fact a piece of black iron with a gold band on either end. The center was inscribed

Obliging Gold-Banded Staff

Weighing 13,500 Pounds

Wukong shrank the staff to the size of a needle and tucked it inside his ear. Satisfied, the Monkey King bade farewell to the Dragon King.

After the Monkey King left, the Dragon King, feeling aggrieved, immediately went to Heaven and complained to the Jade Emperor about Wukong's unwelcome visit. He explained that the Monkey King made demands, caused a disturbance, took away the precious staff of magic iron, and alarmed his subjects. The Dragon King pleaded with the Jade Emperor to subdue Monkey.

The Jade Emperor approved the request and discussed with his heavenly ministers how to bring Monkey under control.

Minister Gold Star came forward. "Your Majesty, why not summon him to Heaven and give him a lowly position so you can keep him under your nose?" he suggested. "If he accepts the position and behaves, he can be promoted. Otherwise, he will be arrested."

The Jade Emperor approved the plan and sent Minister Gold Star to talk to Monkey.

Meanwhile, the Monkey King was on Flowers and Fruit Mountain showing his subjects the treasure he brought back from Water Crystal Palace. Whenever Wukong said, "Big, big, big!" to the iron staff, it grew long enough to scrape the sky and plunge into the earth's core. When he said, "Small, small, small!" the staff shrank to the size of a sewing needle to be tucked into his ear.

The monkeys were thrilled and all of them cheered.

Soon, Minister Gold Star arrived on Flowers and Fruit Mountain. He delivered the Jade Emperor's message to the Monkey King, inviting him to become a sage in Heaven. Wukong readily accepted the offer because he wanted to see what Heaven was like. He ordered the monkeys to keep practicing kung fu and went up to the clouds with Minister Gold Star to travel to Heaven.

Although they left at the same time, the Monkey King's cloud-somersault was so much faster than a normal cloud that Minister Gold Star fell behind.

When Wukong arrived at Heaven's South Gate, the heavenly guards blocked him from entering. As he was about to force his way in, Minister Gold Star arrived and explained to the guards that the Jade Emperor was expecting Monkey. The guards lowered their weapons and let the pair in.

Minister Gold Star led the Monkey King to the Hall of Divine Clouds, the Jade Emperor's throne room. But when they got there, Wukong did not show any respect to the Jade Emperor.

The heavenly ministers were all appalled. "What an unruly Monkey! How disrespectful!"

Minister Gold Star quickly said to the Jade Emperor, "Your Majesty, he is ignorant about court etiquette. Please forgive him."

The Jade Emperor gave a reluctant nod to indicate forgiveness and announced that Monkey was to be the Heavenly Stable Supervisor. Having no idea what rank the title represented, the delighted Monkey King dressed in his official robes, bade Minister Gold Star goodbye, and went to work in the Heavenly Stables.

After Wukong left, the Jade Emperor summoned Heavenly Marshal Hua Guang and ordered him to strictly supervise Monkey. The marshal accepted the command with a bow and left the throne room.

When the Monkey King arrived at the Heavenly Stable, he found all the heavenly horses tied to posts and dispirited. Wukong shook his head, saying, "Is this any way to raise good horses?" He untied them and let them run free.

The heavenly horses enjoyed their freedom immensely. The Monkey King was happy for them. He even jumped into the sky, transformed himself into a raincloud, and showered the horses clean. Because of Wukong's painstaking efforts, the horses were soon healthy and lively, which was very different from before.

One day, Marshal Hua Guang came to inspect Monkey's work. When he saw the horses running free, he yelled, "Who released the horses?"

"Who is shouting here?" the Monkey King snapped. "How dare you?"

"I was sent by the Jade Emperor to supervise you—a lowly horse-keeping official," replied Marshal Hua Guang.

Furious to hear this, Wukong said, "I am the king of Flowers and Fruit Mountain, yet you lured me here to trick me into being your stable boy?" He ripped off his official robe and cap, threw them to Marshal Hua Guang, and walked away.

The more Wukong thought about it, the angrier he became. He retrieved his weapon from his ear, expanded it into a large staff, and fought his way out of Heaven's South Gate. With a cloud-somersault, he returned to Flowers and Fruit Mountain.

The next day at court, the Jade Emperor heard that the offended Monkey King had gone back to his tribe upon realizing how lowly his position was. The Jade Emperor immediately appointed Li Jing, also called King of the Pagoda, as Grand Marshal of Conquering Demons. He made Li's third son, Prince Nezha, a general and told them to lead heavenly soldiers to capture Monkey.

The father and son returned to their residence, organized the army, and made plans for their mission. When everything was set, they led the army out through Heaven's South Gate and descended to Flowers and Fruit Mountain. The first thing that caught their eyes was a huge banner flying in the wind, with the words GREAT SAGE EQUAL TO HEAVEN written on it in large letters.

Li Jing pitched camp and sent his marshal Mighty-Spirit Deity to issue a challenge. The marshal took two giant iron hammers, went to Water Curtain Cave, and shouted to provoke the Monkey King.

"Save your talk, you witless deity!" shouted the furious Monkey King. "Look at my banner. If the Jade Emperor promotes me to a position worthy of the title on my banner, I'll make peace with him. If he does not, I'll bring the fight to his palace."

Mighty-Spirit sneered and swung his iron hammers at the Monkey King. Wukong met him head-on and struck with his iron staff. So powerful was his blow that it smashed the Mighty-Spirit Deity's palm and his esteem.

Mighty-Spirit rumbled with fury, but he was no match for the Monkey King. Wukong plunged his iron staff into the ground and then lowered it toward Mighty-Spirit, immobilizing him and pushing him to the ground. Dozens of small monkeys jumped on him and tortured him with their sharp claws.

Seeing the defeat of Mighty-Spirit, Li Jing ordered his son to take over.

The Monkey King laughed at the prince. "Little prince, how do you dare fight me, when you still have your baby teeth? Go ask the Jade Emperor to recognize me as the Great Sage Equal to Heaven."

Prince Nezha was disgusted. "You monstrous monkey! You'll never be worthy of such a grand title! Meet my spear!"

It was a fierce battle. Nezha shouted "Change!" He turned himself into a warrior with three heads and six arms, each hand holding a weapon, and threw himself at the Monkey King.

Taken aback, Wukong plucked three of his own hairs and turned them into three copies of himself to fight Nezha, while he retreated to safety up in a cloud to watch the fight.

When Nezha realized he had been fooled by the monkey copies, he was so angry that he threw a wheel of fire. Wind and fire engulfed the three monkeys and burned them so completely that it left no trace. He was very proud of his fire trick.

Infuriated to see Nezha rejoicing, the Monkey King transformed into a wheel of fire and whirled toward Nezha. Having no idea whether the wheel was real or not, Nezha stamped on it, burned his feet, and cried out in pain.

When Li Jing saw his son limp back into camp, he was horrified and quickly withdrew the Third Prince and the army to Heaven to get reinforcements.

Looking up at the sky and laughing, the Monkey King and his subjects celebrated their victory.

When Li Jing and Nezha arrived at the Hall of Divine Clouds, the Jade Emperor was enjoying a heavenly show of music and dance. The Phoenix Fairy danced in colorful clouds to ethereal and melodious music.

Li Jing interrupted and reported to the Jade Emperor. "Your Majesty, we have just returned from meeting the monkey tribe," he said. "We were ordered to capture the demonic Monkey, but we didn't expect him to be so powerful that we couldn't win against him. We beg you to send reinforcements with us to complete the mission."

As the Jade Emperor was about to approve the request for reinforcements, Minister Gold Star stepped forward. "Your Majesty, since the demon Monkey has no idea about the rank or status of official positions, why not just give him the fancy title of the Great Sage Equal to Heaven, but without duties or compensation. That would keep him well behaved and in the Heavenly Court, so that both Heaven and Earth can enjoy peace and order."

The Jade Emperor approved the idea and sent Minister Gold Star as his messenger to Flowers and Fruit Mountain. When he landed, he was immediately captured by monkey soldiers. They raised their prize up over their heads and carried him to the Monkey King, shouting, "Your Majesty, we caught a spy!"

Gold Star stood before the Monkey King and said, "Great Sage, the Jade Emperor has learned that you left the Heavenly Stable because you felt the job was beneath you. At the risk of being blamed, I took your request to the Jade Emperor and pleaded on your behalf. Now the Jade Emperor has promised to award you the title of the Great Sage Equal to Heaven and sent me here to invite you back."

"I am *already* the Great Sage Equal to Heaven," scoffed the Monkey King. "Why do I need him to award me the title? I enjoy complete freedom here—more so than in Heaven. No, I'm not going."

Gold Star came up with an idea to overcome the refusal. While complementing the scenery on Flowers and Fruit Mountain, he enticed the Monkey King with talk of the Queen Mother's Orchard of Immortal Peaches. He suggested that the Jade Emperor would put Wukong in charge of the Orchard. The bait worked. The Monkey King was fascinated by the idea and returned to Heaven.

The Jade Emperor pronounced Monkey "Great Sage Equal to Heaven." In his new official robes as Great Sage, Monkey followed Minister Gold Star's directions and headed for the Orchard of Immortal Peaches in a cloud-somersault.

Upon learning that the Great Sage was to manage the orchard, the land spirit politely told him about the peach trees. "Eating the peaches from this orchard, can make a person as immortal as Heaven and Earth and the sun and moon."

As a peach lover like every monkey, the Great sage was thrilled to hear this. When he found half of the peaches on an old tree already ripe, he took off his robes and climbed the tree to enjoy the peaches.

The land spirit quickly stopped him. "Great Sage, you cannot eat them now. The peaches must be saved until the Queen Mother of Jade Lake holds the Grand Peach Feast."

With a frown, the Great Sage climbed down and thought of a plan. "I see. Well, you go and wait outside while I take a nap here." Once the land spirit left, Wukong wasted no time climbing back up the tree and feasting on the largest ripe peaches.

When he was too full to eat any more, he shrank himself until he was only a few inches long, lay down on a tree branch, covered himself with a peach leaf, and fell asleep.

As the day for the Grand Peach Feast approached, the Queen Mother sent seven fairies to the orchard to pick peaches. When they arrived at the entrance, the land spirit told them to report to the Great Sage before they could enter. But the land spirit searched the orchard and couldn't find him anywhere. Unable to disobey the Queen Mother's order, he had to let them in.

When the seven fairies entered the garden to pick peaches, they were disappointed to find only a few fruits and they were not even ripe yet. They had no idea that the good ones had been eaten by the Great Sage. Finally they found a big red and white peach and lowered the branch to pick it.

It turned out that the big peach was Monkey in disguise. He was awakened by a fairy's touch and changed back into his real form. Alarmed, the fairies scattered. When he realized they had come to prepare for the Grand Peach Feast, Wukong asked who had been invited. The fairies listed all of the guests, but the Great Sage Equal to Heaven was not on the list.

The Great Sage was furious. The frightened fairies immediately fled on their clouds. Wukong shouted "Halt! Stay!" and froze the fairies in midair. He raced on a cloud to Jade Lake where the Queen Mother was.

Soon, he saw colorful lights glowing deep in the misty clouds. Below was a beautiful crystal-clear lake, home to many jade carvings. Spring water flowed from a carved jade hole, and at the heart of the spring was a night pearl. Monkey flew to the pearl and looked around the lake.

He saw the Palace of Jade Lake richly decorated with lanterns, flowers, and ribbons. The whole palace was wreathed in sweet mists and fragrances. The stewards brought big jars of heavenly wine, and servants were busy setting tables. Wukong became invisible, entered the palace, and found tables spread with an abundance of enticing delicacies, nectar, and wines.

The mouth-watering scene made him long to enjoy the feast undisturbed. He plucked several hairs from his body, chewed them into pieces, spat them out, and commanded, "Change!" Instantly, they became sleep-inducing insects and flew into the faces of the people, who immediately passed out and fell to the ground.

Taking advantage of the quiet, Monkey transformed back into his normal shape, sat at the highest seat at the table, and enjoyed the dishes and wines to his heart's content.

The Great Sage became very drunk and suddenly remembered all the monkeys on Flowers and Fruit Mountain. Plucking another hair, Wukong turned it into a bottomless sack, and filled it with wine and heavenly delicacies from the table, so he could share them with his subjects.

Tying the sack around his waist, the Great Sage headed back to Flowers and Fruit Mountain. But because he drank too much wine, he took a wrong turn and accidentally arrived at the palace of the Taoist Master.

When he realized he had gone the wrong way, Monkey thought, "I might as well visit the Taoist Master as long as I'm here." Wukong toured the palace and couldn't find the Master even in the potions room. In fact, the Master happened not to be home at the time. In the potions room the Great Sage saw a bronze bell near the furnace which gave off colorful rays of light. Monkey opened it and saw a gourd inside.

He shook the gourd gently and found it full of golden elixir. "This is the most precious treasure to the immortals!" Monkey exclaimed in delight. "Let me try some while the Master is not home." After pouring out the elixir capsules, he swallowed them all and began shining with heavenly light. He was also completely sober and thought, *Oh no! I'll be in big trouble when they find out what I did. I should leave right now.*

Wukong made himself invisible and returned to his tribe in a cloud-somersault. His subjects were thrilled to see him return. He emptied the bottomless sack and let them feast on the heavenly delicacies and wine.

The Queen Mother became furious when she found her banquet hall wrecked, the tables and chairs overturned, the plates and cups in disarray, and all of the people snoring. Just then, the seven fairies recovered from Monkey's spell and reported to the Queen Mother that the Great Sage had eaten all the good peaches, immobilized the fairies, and disappeared.

The Queen Mother immediately reported the incident to the Jade Emperor. The Taoist Master also went to the Jade Emperor to report that the Great Sage had stolen all his precious elixir pills. The angry Jade Emperor ordered Li Jing and Prince Nezha to lead the Four Heavenly Kings and 100,000 heavenly soldiers to Flowers and Fruit Mountain to subdue Monkey. They brought heavenly nets to help them catch him.

A monkey patrol reported to their king that the heavenly army was on its way. The Monkey King quickly assembled his army in battle formation and went out to meet the enemy.

The Southern Heavenly King rushed to the front of the battle, recited a spell, and split his sword into a thousand swords that shot toward the Monkey King. Calmly, Wukong plucked out a hair and turned it into a thousand shields to fend off the swords.

Next came the Eastern Heavenly King with his lute. He played the instrument, send-ing out enchanting music that made the Monkey King and his soldiers dizzy.

The Northern Heavenly King's weapon was a magical umbrella that produced a thick fog. Suddenly a gust of wind sucked the Great Sage and his soldiers into the umbrella. The Northern King took back his magic weapon, laughing loudly.

Inside the umbrella, the Great Sage woke up and tried to break it open with his iron staff, but it stayed intact. So he pulled out a hair, turned it into a diamond drill, and bored several big holes in the umbrella. Light coming through the holes woke the monkeys up, and they all escaped.

Wukong grabbed the Eastern Heavenly King's lute and jangled the strings, plucking them randomly. With a loud *twang*, the strings snapped. With their magical weapons broken, the Eastern and Northern Heavenly Kings panicked and fled.

The Western Heavenly King quickly released a fierce, poisonous serpent to attack the Great Sage. On the snake's head, a pearl flashed with cold light, and the creature exhaled toxic mist. After they fought for a while, Wukong realized that the pearl had secret powers. When he found an opening, he tore the pearl from the snake's head, and the serpent died at once.

When Erlang, an Immortal Master and nephew of the Jade Emperor, saw the four Heavenly Kings defeated, he and his Howling Celestial Dog threw themselves into the fight against the Great Sage. Erlang's blade clashed with the Monkey King's gold-banded iron staff.

The rest of the heavenly army took the opportunity to raid Flowers and Fruit Mountain. But the monkeys were waiting near the Water Curtain Cave to ambush them. When the heavenly soldiers arrived, the monkeys aimed the waterfall to spray at their enemies, using its force as a weapon. The heavenly army retreated but as the monkeys scrambled away, they tripped on vines and fell.

The heavenly army regrouped and launched a new attack on the monkeys with arrows and fire. The monkeys were no match for the soldiers and retreated. Some jumped into mountain streams and some sought shelter between rocks.

Seeing this, the Great Sage lost interest in fighting. He only wanted to protect his subjects, so he fled. But Erlang chased him, staying close at his heels. Hoping to escape, the Monkey King turned himself into a sparrow. Right away, Erlang changed into a sparrowhawk and headed straight toward him.

Thinking quickly, the Great Sage plunged into a mountain stream and turned into a small fish to swim away, only to have Erlang transform into an egret that stretched forward and tried to catch the Monkey King with its beak.

The Great Sage rode the stream over a cliff and rolled himself onto the ground where he became a land-spirit temple, with his eyes as windowpanes and his mouth as the door. Not knowing what to do with his tail, Wukong turned it into a flagpole behind the temple.

When Erlang saw it, he could not help laughing. "What kind of temple would have a flagpole behind it?" Looking with the all-seeing third eye on his forehead, Erlang saw the Monkey King in his true form.

From high in a cloud, the Taoist Master watched Erlang and the Great Sage resume their fight. This was the same Master whose elixir Wukong had stolen. Realizing that Erlang would not win, the Taoist Master rolled up his sleeves, removed a gold and steel cutting ring from his arm, and hurled it down to the earth, hitting the Monkey King right on his head. Erlang's Howling Celestial Dog jumped up and bit the Great Sage's leg, making it easier for the others to swarm in and capture him.

When they returned to Heaven, the Jade Emperor ordered that Monkey be tied to the Demon-Subduing Post on the Demon-Execution Platform to be punished. No matter what they tried—slicing with knives, chopping with axes, stabbing with spears, slashing with swords, burning with fire, or striking him with thunderbolts—it had no effect whatsoever on Wukong. The Jade Emperor had no choice but to have him thrown into the Taoist Master's alchemy furnace for forty-nine days to extract the elixir from him.

At the end of this time, the Taoist Master thought that the fire must have burned Monkey long enough to get the elixir out of him.

Who knew that the Great Sage would be in the furnace unharmed and improved?

When he opened the alchemy furnace, the Master was shocked to see Monkey rubbing his eyes.

Not only was the Great Sage healthy, he was endowed with all-seeing powers. When he heard the furnace open, Wukong jumped out, kicked it over, and escaped.

The Great Sage took the iron staff from his ear, expanded it to his desired size, and fought his way from east to west to the Hall of Divine Clouds. There, the Monkey King knocked down pillars and beams.

Publisher's Note

All books in our The Irrepressible Monkey King series are based on the Chinese novel *Journey to the West*. Written in the 1500s during the Ming Dynasty by Wu Cheng'en, *Journey to the West* is one of the Four Great Classical Novels of Chinese literature. The story mixes myths and folklore with historical events from the 7th century. There are a few well-known translations into English, some of which are condensed, while others are complete. This book is a new translation into English from an abridged Chinese-language version of *Journey to the West*.

The original text of this work was written in Chinese. The translator, editor, and publisher have made every effort to ensure that the English-language version is as accurate as possible and in keeping with the artistic intent of the author. Because this work reflects a different culture, some of the ideas and attitudes may be unfamiliar to the English-language audience.